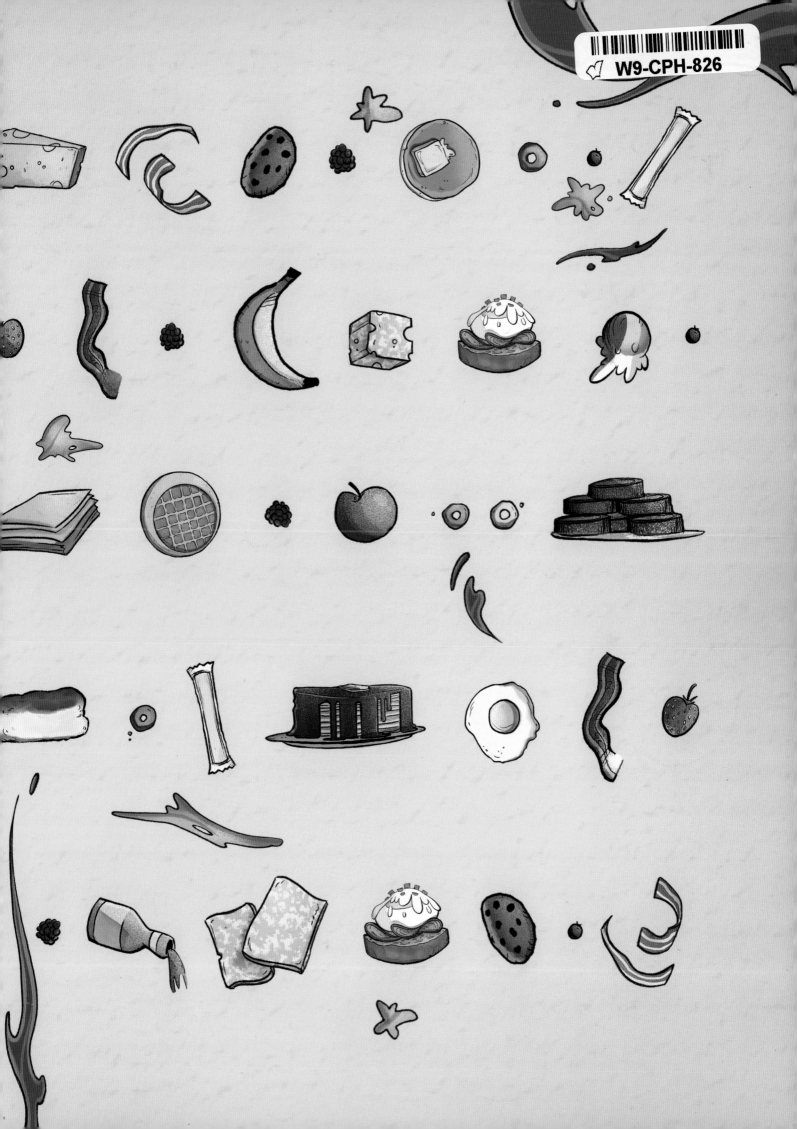

TO MY TWO FAVORITE PEOPLE
TO SHARE A MEAL WITH
SIGGI AND JETT

This is A.J.

This is Theo
(he's A.J.'s best friend)

Today is Saturday!
A.J.'s favorite day of the week. Come see why...

But nothing ever goes as planned.

The kitchen's a strange place,
as you can tell by the look on my face.
So strange, there's already a feast,
breakfast being served by creatures and beasts.

When my mom cooks breakfast, everything seems to be fine,

which tends to be true...

FIFTY SILLY FISHES,
SWIMMING IN THE DISHES.
THIS CANNOT BE RIGHT.
WHY ARE ANIMALS IN
THE KITCHEN?

A panda frying bacon.

A rooster baking hen.
Geese buttering duck.

By the time
I make breakfast,
it will be time

for my lunch.

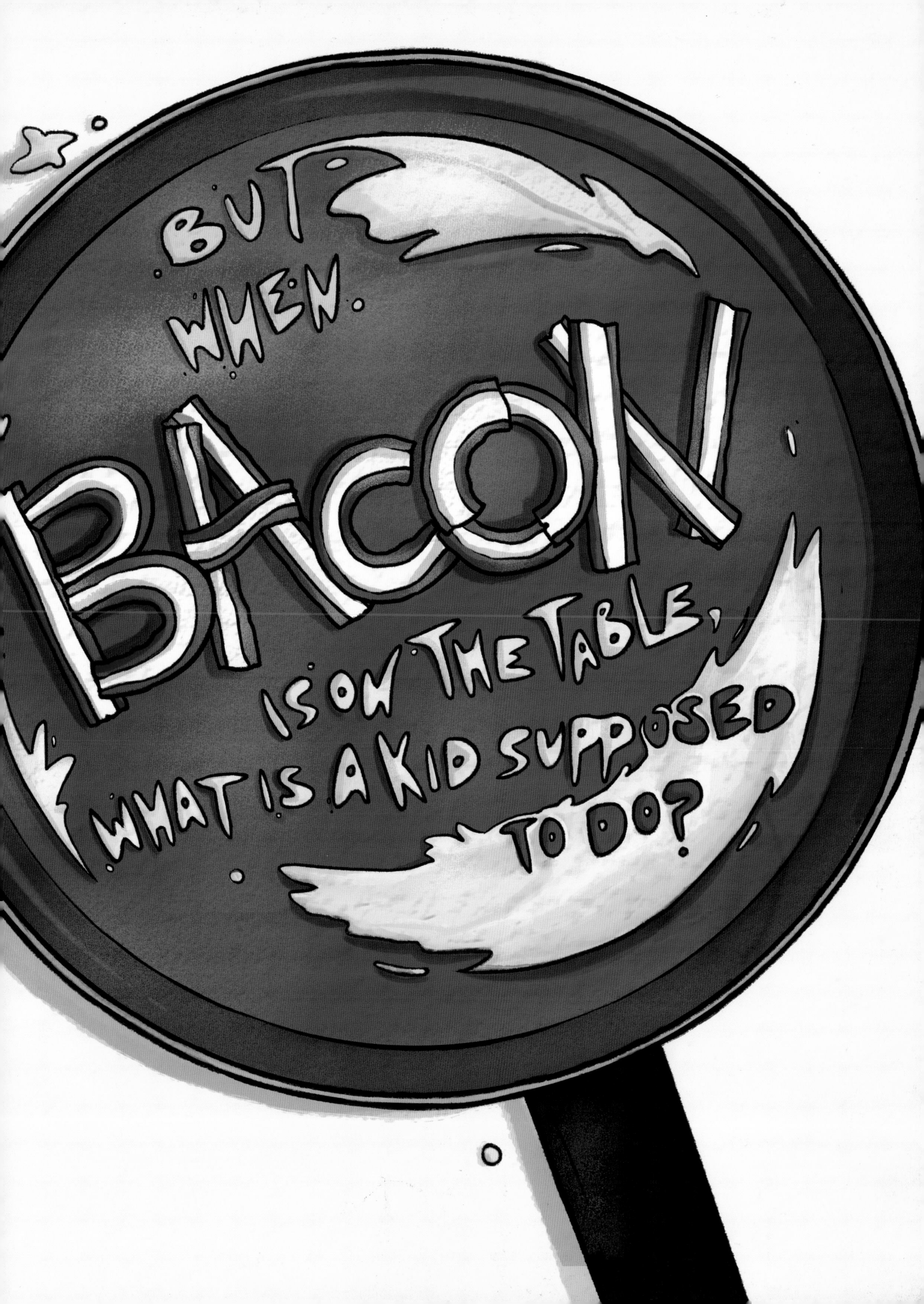
BUT WHEN
BACON
IS ON THE TABLE,
WHAT IS A KID SUPPOSED TO DO?

THERE'S A COUPLE OF THINGS ABOUT BREAKFAST THAT NO ONE IN THE WORLD KNOWS.

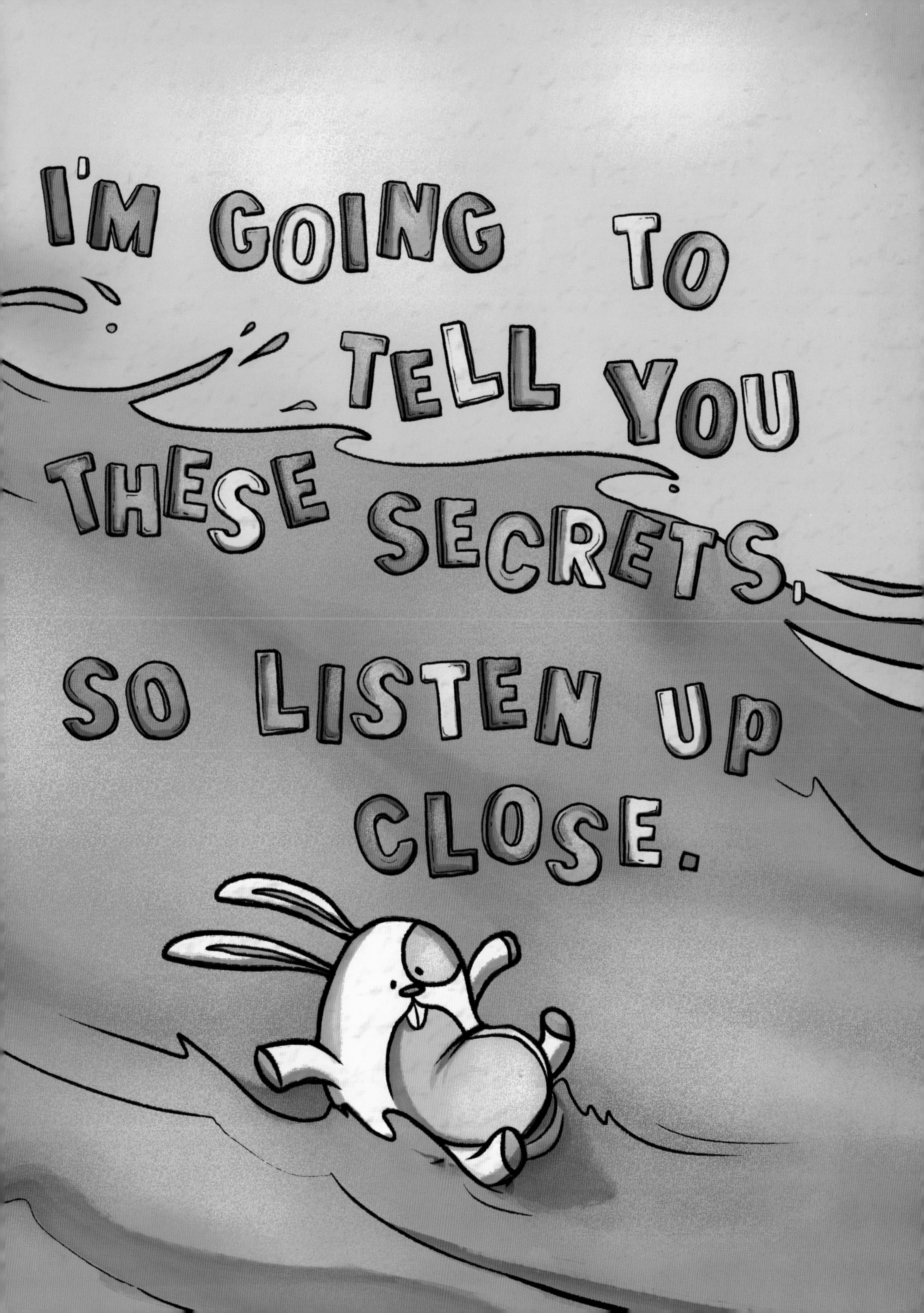
I'M GOING TO TELL YOU THESE SECRETS, SO LISTEN UP CLOSE.

Pancakes can swim.

Eggs Benedict loves
to work out anywhere,
not just in a gym,

and crêpes are creepy,
tiny mustached men.

Eggs being scrambled are just eggs running around the pan.

Barstools standing at the bar

watching highlights, arguing over calls.

So I did
the thing that
most parents hate

and screamed,,
"MOOOOOOOM!"
really loud 'til I heard her awake.

Then I asked her nicely
to come fix me a plate,
Full of all the delicious things
that she loves to make.

I shrugged and smiled.

visit the Hey A.J. website!
(www.HeyAJ.com)

You're invited to join me and Theo and all my
crazy animal friends on our brand new website
(www.HeyAJ.com). Yes, the Jamaican Giraffe will
be there (his name is Wilbur by the way) plus lots
of my other friends as well. Log on and join us.

We'll be telling stories, playing puzzles and
games, and making a mess with our imaginations.

We'll wait for you. Because a party isn't a party
without you.

See You Soon!

Download my interactive App. (Available Now) So we can hang out any time you want.

My App is awesome!!!!! There's animation, music, games, sound effects, narrations and so many more fun things for us to do:

- We can float down the amazing SMOOTHIE river
- Scramble eggs
- Play hide & seek with Theo
- And practice karate with ninja waffles

Search Hey A.J. in the app Stores

www.theimaginationagency.com - www.heyaj.com
First published in USA by THE IMAGINATION AGENCY in 2017
ISBN: 978-0-9969820-4-7

Book design Digital Leaf - Printed in China

Marty loves breakfast. In fact he eats breakfast for breakfast, sometimes for lunch and for dinner as often as possible.

He lives in a magical house in Chicago with his wife and daughter, in which all of the creatures and toys come to life, especially when there's food on the table.

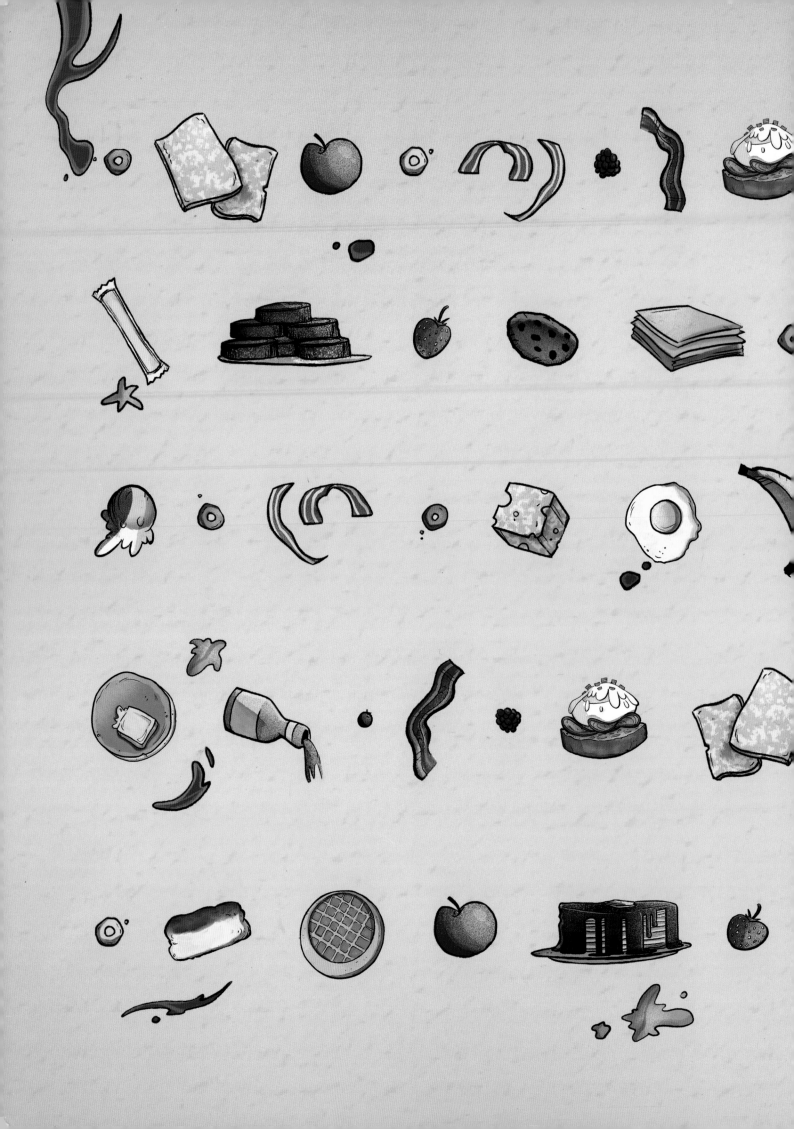